"If you want to go fast, go alone.
If you want to go far, go together."

African proverb

SEAN TACKLES
LONDON

By

TANYA PREMINGER

Illustrations

ELETTRA CUDIGNOTTO

To Teddy, who walks with me the path of life

Contents

TANYA PREMINGER

London Eye

It's a beautiful August day in London. Daddy, Mommy, and Sean cling to each other as tourists swarm around them at the foot of the London Eye.

"No, Sean, I am not getting on that thing!" Daddy exclaims.

"Please, do it with us!" pleads Sean, fidgeting with excitement.

"You and Mommy go ahead. I'll wait for you down here on the grass," says Daddy as he tilts his head back and gazes nervously at the huge metal structure of the most famous Ferris wheel in the world. The glass Ferris wheel cars shine in the sun as they rotate slowly against the cloudless blue sky.

Daddy feels dizzy.

"No way..." he mumbles.

1

"Daddy, it's safe! Look - all those people are doing it." Sean waves at the long line of visitors who wait patiently to get tickets.

"I don't like heights," insists Daddy.

"But you can't let your fear control you! I'm scared too, of going to the FC Barcelona soccer camp," Sean confesses. "Still, I'm doing it anyway, because it's important to me."

"This is not important to me," Daddy says. "I could live without going on this Ferris wheel."

"It will be a great experience for us, Daddy. It will unite us as a family," says Sean with a wink at Mommy.

Mommy laughs.

"Look, the cars are closed," Sean continues. "So you can't fall! I'm only nine years old, and I'm not afraid to go."

A group of excited teenage girls in robes and white hijabs pass by. They've just gotten off the Ferris wheel, and they are giggling and chatting in excitement.

"Can't you try, Daddy? It's our annual vacation. We crossed the Atlantic just to be here!" says Mommy.

"I say we save money on my ticket," Daddy replies.

⚽ ⚽ ⚽

"Wow! We are so high up!" Sean calls out.

Mommy and Sean are observing the skyline through the window of their Ferris wheel car. Squinting their eyes against the bright sun, they look at London's famous landmarks - boats sailing on

the River Thames, Westminster Abbey and Hyde Park, London Bridge and Big Ben.

They shuffle along the window, switching places with other delighted tourists. Mommy takes numerous pictures of the famous clock tower with her cell phone.

As they ascend to the highest point of the Ferris wheel, an excited murmur in many languages fills the car.

"The people below look like ants!" cries Sean.

"Look, there is Daddy!" Mommy exclaims as she spots him sitting on a patch of grass with a plastic cup of beer in his hand.

"Mommy, what if I'm afraid to play in the soccer camp?" Sean's thoughts skip to tomorrow.

"What is there to be afraid of?" Mommy wonders. "You are a talented soccer player. You'll be playing with other kids your age. So what if they come from all over the world? Soccer is an international language. And anyway, it doesn't matter if you are the best on the field or not - you'll be there to have fun."

"I'm sure I'll play better than the other kids," Sean says. "The coach will notice me and sign me up right away."

"Well, I don't think it works that way," smiles Mommy.

"But you said there is going to be a coach there from the Barcelona Youth Academy!"

"Yes, that's what the brochure said," Mommy confirms.

"So he will remember me and tell the Barcelona club they should buy me."

"They don't buy nine-year-old boys," Mommy tells him. "And

besides, you are not going to the camp to compete - you are going there to learn."

As they start their descent to the ground, two Asian toddlers wave at them cheerfully from the next car. Sean waves back.

"Mommy, do you think that when I'm a professional soccer player, I should ask for my salary in euros, or in dollars? Because I heard the euro price fell recently."

Mommy chuckles. "There's still a lot of time before we need to worry about that. Let's take it step by step."

King's Cross Underground

It's morning rush hour in the King's Cross underground station. Daddy, Mommy, and Sean stand confused at a crossroads, in front of a huge London Underground map - a tangled web of colored lines.

"To the right! We need to take the yellow line," says Daddy.

"No, we need to take the purple line! Daddy, you know that you're not good with directions," Mommy says as she inspects the map closely.

All around them, people dressed in London's sleek style hurry to work.

"What are you talking about? We need to get off at Harrow on the Hill Station," Daddy insists.

"Exactly! That's why we need to take the purple line. Look!" Mommy runs her finger along the route of the underground line on the map.

"I don't need a map," says Daddy stubbornly. "I've lived in this city before, remember?"

"That was ages ago," Mommy reminds him, raising her eyebrows, "and frankly, I think that whenever you think you should go one way, you should actually take the opposite direction, and you'll be all right." She smiles at her own joke.

"Very funny!" Daddy is irritated.

"Make up your minds!" Sean interrupts with a cry. "We are going to be late for the camp registration!"

Mommy decides to take action.

"Left corridor! After me!" She grabs Sean's hand and pulls him after her as she rushes down the underground pedestrian tunnel. Daddy follows suit reluctantly. They make their way through the rushing crowd, as they hear the deafening squeal of a train approaching the station.

The train stops. Panting, they squeeze in the sliding doors, grabbing the only seat available. Mommy and Daddy let Sean sit, while they stand next to him, holding the top rail.

"We have another hour and a half until the registration. We'll get there on time," Mommy reassures everyone as the train starts moving.

"What did you eat for breakfast, Sean?" Daddy asks.

Sean shrugs his shoulders guiltily.

"He refused to eat everything I offered him," Mommy says.

"That's not good, Sean!" Daddy exclaims, "How are you going to last the day? You've got six hours of training ahead of you."

"He was too nervous to eat," Mommy explains.

"I'm not nervous at all," objects Sean nervously.

Mommy runs her fingertips through Sean's hair in a comforting gesture. "I packed sandwiches in his bag," she says. "Did you brush your teeth this morning, Sean?"

Sean shakes his head. "You were rushing me."

"That's terrible." Mommy turns to Daddy. "Daddy, you've got to say something."

Daddy takes a deep breath. "Sean, if you don't brush your teeth every day, they will rot, and you will have a mouthful of cavities, which will end up costing you a fortune."

"So what?"' smiles Sean. "I will be a professional soccer player. I will be able to afford any surgery I want."

The train slows to a stop.

"Watch the gap between the train and the platform," a deep male voice advises over the PA system. Passengers walk in and out. The seat next to Sean frees up, and Daddy offers it to Mommy as the train begins to move again.

"How much longer?" grumbles Sean.

"Why did you book us a place so far away from the soccer camp?" inquires Daddy, glancing at his wife.

"Oh, you guys...! Stop whining," says Mommy, irritated. "We wanted to stay close to all the attractions in the city center. It wasn't easy to find something inexpensive."

The train emerges from the underground into a bright suburban London morning. Rows of residential houses with small backyards and well-kept gardens pass by outside the windows. Sean slips a hand into Daddy's pocket and grabs his cell phone.

Daddy is not happy with this, but he lets Sean play with it. They pass a few more train stops.

"I want to get a haircut like this one." Sean turns the cell phone screen toward his parents and shows them a photo of Lionel Messi.

"A haircut? Your hair looks just fine. You can't wait until we're back at home?" Mommy is puzzled.

"No. I need this hair today." Sean waves the cell phone in the air.

"A bleached Mohawk?" Daddy shakes his head in disapproval.

"It will definitely get you a lot of attention," says Mommy, bewildered.

"What's wrong with attention? I like attention," smiles Sean.

"You should want attention because of your soccer-playing skills, not because of your hair," Mommy objects.

"Because of both! Please, Mommy, Daddy, I want that haircut!"

"And I want to be a rock star," Daddy smirks.

Mommy glances at the underground map for the hundredth time. "We're getting off at the next station," she warns.

"Personally, I still think we are going in the wrong direction," murmurs Daddy.

Learn To Play
The Barca Way

Mommy, Daddy, and Sean are hurrying up a winding asphalt country road. Georgian houses are nestled in greenery on either side, their brown bricks covered in moss.

As they approach the top of the hill, magnificent vistas of the English countryside become visible between the houses, and rolling hills and meadows sparkle in the sun all the way to the horizon. Mommy points out the famous Wembley Stadium to the southeast.

At the village center, they see a church and the numerous buildings of the Harrow School, surrounded by immaculate lawns and neatly trimmed hedges. The main building dominates the peak of the hill, with massive ornamental wooden doors and steeples that protrude into the sky.

"You know, I read that Harry Potter was filmed here. This was the Hogwarts School of Witchcraft and Wizardry," Mommy tells Sean.

"Who cares?" says Sean impatiently. "Where's the camp? We are going to be late!"

"We should've taken the bus," adds Daddy.

"But it says here that it's only a ten-minute walk." Mommy checks the camp brochure she's holding once again.

"Let's ask those people - it looks like they might know." Daddy glances at an Asian family walking ahead of them. The parents hold the same soccer camp brochures, and their two kids - twins - are dressed in matching FC Barcelona sportswear.

Daddy approaches them and asks where the camp is. The couple smile and point to a road down the hill.

"Where are you from?" Mommy asks them curiously.

"We are from Taiwan."

"Taiwan? Wow! And you came to London just for the camp?"

"Yes, our kids are big fans of soccer and Lionel Messi. Where are you from?" the father asks.

"We are from the USA."

"That's a long way, too!" the mother exclaims.

Finally, they find the facility where the camp registration is taking place - a modern-day building that is a part of a sports complex. Yellow and red FC Barcelona banners mark the entrance, and excited parents and kids rush in and out of the glass doors.

Mommy, Daddy, and Sean gaze at them and try to guess which

country each family is from.

Each child approaches the registration desk, where they get an identification bracelet and a shiny red FCB school uniform.

Sean goes to the dressing room with the other kids to try his red uniform on, gesturing discreetly to his parents to wait right by the door.

Once all the kids are registered, the parents and kids follow the administration team outside, past lavish lawns and old oak trees, to the soccer field where the opening ceremony takes place.

Each kid's name is read out loud and they are required to step forward and join their respective team. The teams are named after FC Barcelona players: "Messi," "Neymar," "Pique," "Suarez," and so on. Sean is called forward to join the "Iniesta" team.

Once all the kids are standing in orderly lines on the grass, the camp manager steps in front of the crowd to deliver a speech.

"Welcome to the FC Barcelona official summer camp in London. It's great to see you all here," he addresses the crowd of proud parents and anxious kids. "You came here to learn to play the Barca way. At this camp, we will teach you what that means. You will get to know the Barcelona tactics and the methodology that helps the team to win games. Five days of hard work are ahead of you."

He pauses for dramatic effect.

"And now, I would like to introduce a special guest from Spain, who will be heading up the coaching team this week. Let's hear it for Mr. Diego Alfaro, the head coach from the La Masia Youth Soccer

Academy in Barcelona. He will share a few words with you."

A cheerful man with unruly dark curly hair steps to the front of the crowd and the parents applaud enthusiastically.

"Good day! Welcome to the FC Barcelona soccer camp!" Diego says with a heavy Spanish accent. "Do you know what's special about FC Barcelona's tactics? I will tell you - it's teamwork. Playing in unity, as one. You don't play for yourself; you play for the team. One for all, all for one! It is not important if you score. It's important if your team wins or loses. Passing is more important than shooting. Smarts and creativity are more important than physical power. This is the Barça way. Let's get started!"

The Barca anthem starts playing and everybody joins in the chorus: "Barca, Barca, Baaaaaaaarca!"

Each team's coach leads his kids to their spot on the soccer field. Some of the parents disperse, while others seat themselves on the margins of the lawn where they can watch the action. Sean gestures to Mommy and Daddy to stay close by.

The "Iniesta" team kids gather around their coach, an amiable young man with a trendy beard.

"Hi, I'm Benji, and I will be your coach this week. I'm from Tottenham, here in London. Let me know if I'm speaking too quickly - I know many of you are not from England."

The kids nod in agreement.

"To start with, I would like each kid to say their name, which country they are from, and who their favorite Barca player is. Okay? Let's go."

"I am Neil, from the USA. I love Messi," a tall blond boy tanned complexion says.

"My name is Shira. I come from Brazil. I love Neymar," follows a girl with a ponytail.

"Floris, from Holland. Suarez is the best!"

"Sean, USA. Messi is the best!" murmurs Sean timidly.

"Howard, Taiwan, Messi," says the first of the Taiwanese twins Sean met earlier.

"Mathew, Taiwan, Messi," adds his twin.

"But those are English names," interjects Neil.

"Yes, we have English names and also Taiwanese names," mutters Howard.

"And what are your Taiwanese names?" asks Benji with a smile.

"Chih-Hao and Chih-Liang."

"Interesting. Chi-ha...hu?" Benji tries to repeat the name. "I think we will use your English names. Okay?"

Howard nods his head in approval.

"Great. Let's carry on," says Benji.

"Paul, UK, Messi," says the small boy next in line.

"Oman, from Jordan. Iniesta."

"Raymar, Saint Lucia. I love Pique."

"Saint Lucia? Where's that?" wonders Paul.

"It's in the Caribbean! Duh!" Neil says mockingly.

The rest of the kids on the team continue introducing themselves, listing countries from all over the globe.

"Now we are ready to start with the first drill," says Benji when

Listen up, kids. I will divide you into two
ellow. We've got white and yellow bibs right
at a pile of soccer equipment. "Each team
ards, two midfielders, two defenders, and a

Benji counts the kids and realizes he doesn't have an even number.

"One player will be a joker. He doesn't belong to a team. When he receives the ball, he passes it back to the team who gave it to him," Benji amends. "You will form attacks and go for the goal, but you must make at least two exchanges with the ball during an attack, otherwise your goal doesn't count. You got it? At least two passes in an attack. You look at the field, you look at your teammates, you check your options, and you find the pass. Sound good?"

The kids nod their heads.

"Neil will be the captain of the Yellow team, and Floris of the White team. Let's go!" Benji calls out.

Sean feels butterflies in his stomach and his heart beats fast in his chest.

Disappointed that he wasn't chosen to be the captain, he searches for Mommy and Daddy for reassurance. They wave to him from the far end of the lawn.

Sean puts on a yellow bib and is assigned to be a forward. The Taiwanese kids and Shira are Yellow players as well. Howard is assigned to be their goalie.

The game begins.

At first, the kids play hesitantly, but soon enough they get into the sport they love and immerse themselves in the game. Paul, the English boy from the White team, turns out to be a big problem. He's quick and fearless, and he dribbles easily past the Yellow team's defense all the way to the goal. Face to face with Howard, he slides a quick left leg kick and scores.

"What are you doing? You can't protect a three-foot goal?!" Neil, who has chased Paul to the goal, blurts at Howard.

Howard frowns.

"No goal!" calls Benji from the sidelines. "What did we say we are working on? Passes! Teamwork! There was no exchange - so no goal. Continue."

The struggle goes on, but the teams are matched equally and their attacks end up without goals.

But then, the ball is captured by the Yellows. Shira passes to Sean. Sean dribbles quickly forward, sweat trickling down his back.

"Check your options! Look at the field!" Benji calls.

Sean hesitates as he scans his surroundings, looking for free players.

"Whites, where's your defense?" Benji yells to the opposing team. "Where's his shade?"

Paul moves in Sean's direction. As he approaches, Sean passes hurriedly to Neil, but the ball slides on his foot, and he shoots too far. Neil lunges ahead, slides on the grass feet-first, and manages

to touch the ball at the last second, diverting it into the Whites' goal.

"Goal! Goal!" Neil shouts. He springs back to his feet and does a celebratory dance.

"Good job! Beautiful goal!" calls Diego Alfaro, the Spanish coach, who happens to be passing by at that moment.

"Great attack, Neil!" adds Benji. "But when you celebrate, you've got to do it together with your team. Remember – soccer is teamwork. Celebrate together!"

Neil runs to his teammates and the Yellows celebrate their victory with a group hug and high-fives.

"He saw me! Diego saw my goal!" cries Neil excitedly as his hand meets Sean's in a high-five. "He's gonna sign me up for La Masia in Barcelona!"

The Red Bus Game

Crammed against the Buckingham Palace fence among a crowd of enthusiastic tourists, Mommy, Daddy, and Sean are trying to get a peek at the royal guards. Mommy sticks her cell phone between the railings, attempting to get a good picture. The guards stand motionless as their famous red jackets and tall black bearskin hats shine in the bright sun.

"Mommy, this is boring. They don't move," whines Sean.

"That's the point, Sean," explains Mommy. "They only move when they change guards."

"Let's go shopping now. I need new cleats." Sean turns from the railing.

"New cleats? What's wrong with the cleats you have now?" asks Daddy.

"I say we go to the London Dungeon," suggests Mommy as they start making their way through the crowd away from the palace.

Daddy disagrees. "Sean wouldn't like the London Dungeon. It's too gruesome."

"You think? But it's a kids' attraction. I want him to see a bit of

London's history, to learn how people lived here centuries ago. After all, this was the celebrated capital of the British Empire," Mommy says.

They walk along a broad avenue, surrounded by elegant flower gardens.

"Let's go to Notting Hill," suggests Daddy.

"Notting Hill?" wonders Sean.

"It used to be my neighborhood. I can show you where I lived. And there are cool coffee shops there, bars, thrift shops, and

Portobello Market. Lots of fun," Daddy replies.

"When did you live in London?" asks Sean.

"It was before I met your mommy. I was a musician," Daddy says with a nostalgic smile.

"I don't want Notting Hill! I want shopping!" concludes Sean.

Mommy checks the map in her hand. "The London Dungeon is not far. We can walk there."

"I don't want to walk. I'm tired. My whole body hurts," moans Sean. "I played soccer for six hours today."

Daddy looks at Mommy. "The kid is tired. You can't drag us on a tour now."

Mommy sighs, exasperated. "But how often do we get the chance to visit London? I want us to see the city."

"Mommy, we are a team! You need to think about your teammates first," argues Sean.

"I am!" Mommy replies.

"I know what!" calls Daddy. "Let's just hop on the first bus that comes along and see where it takes us! There's a bus stop right here."

"Daddy... I don't know about this idea..." Mommy shakes her head disapprovingly and opens up the map again.

"No map!" Daddy yanks it from her hand. "Let's just go."

"No map!" Sean backs him up, delighted.

"If we take bus number forty, we will get to the London Dungeon." Mommy won't give up.

"No, we take the first bus that comes!" calls Daddy.

On the upper floor of the double-decker bus, Sean is comfortably propped against the window at the front. He is holding the rail as the bus winds through London's streets. Elegant eighteenth-century townhouses, modern-day glass and steel buildings, coffee shops, and chic stores pass before his eyes.

"When do we get off?" asks Mommy, wondering where they are.

"When we see something interesting," Daddy replies with a grin.

They arrive at a shopping district. Stores are lined up on both sides of the street, selling everything one could imagine, from clothing to food to cosmetics, and everything in between. All the familiar big brands showcase their tempting merchandise. Throngs of people walk the pavements.

"So many people! So many stores! So many buses!" Sean cries in excitement.

He watches red double-deckers buses and taxis crawl up the street in the bumper-to-bumper traffic.

"Mommy, I'm playing a game," Sean says. "I'm counting the buses. If ten buses drive by in a row, I win. If a car slips in, I have to start over. A taxi is a joker."

"Cool! I like that game," Mommy approves.

"And if I win, you have to give me twenty pounds for shopping," declares Sean.

"Twenty pounds? Seriously?" exclaims Daddy.

"Fine," agrees Mommy. "But if you lose, you wash the dishes for two weeks."

Daddy laughs.

"One week." Sean tries to improve the terms.

"Okay," says Mommy, seeing that spotting ten buses in a row will be a challenge.

"And if we see a hairdresser, we have to stop and get my hair cut," adds Sean cunningly. "Those are the rules."

"I didn't agree to the hairdresser part," Mommy protests.

"You are the worst mommy in the world!" Sean cries. "But just so you know, I will always love you anyway."

Sean starts counting the vehicles waiting for a traffic light. "Six…seven….a car!"

"I think I know where we're going," Daddy announces suddenly.

"Daddy, do you think that boy, Neil, is good?" Sean asks, paying no attention to what Daddy just said.

"The tall blond guy? I noticed him. He's got good technique."

"But Daddy, I have good technique, too. And I'm very precise. I can hit an exact spot with the ball from thirty feet away."

"I know that, Sean."

"And Neil plays solo," adds Sean. "He is not a team player."

"Well, sometimes it's okay to play solo," says Daddy. "Sometimes, depending on the situation, you have to be decisive, take a risk, and just go for it with everything you've got."

Sean huffs. "That's not the Barcelona way! Teamwork is more

important. Diego said so."

"I think this is Oxford Street!" Mommy interrupts, watching the throngs of people on the pavements

Their bus is standing in traffic in front of a sports store with the latest soccer cleats designs displayed in the window.

"Daddy, look! All my favorite sports stores in a row! I love this city! I love it!" exclaims Sean.

"It's too crowded for me. All this chaos makes me feel anxious," Daddy grimaces.

"Let's go in that sports store! C'mon, Mom, Dad! "

"But you didn't win any money yet," Mommy reminds him.

"Never mind, we will only window-shop. We won't buy anything – at least not yet," urges Sean.

"No! We are not getting off here," Daddy says.

"Mommy!" Sean tries.

"No, Sean, no shopping now."

The bus halts at a bus stop and they hear the whir of the door-opening system.

Sean stands up with a cunning look on his face.

"Sit back down right now!" calls Daddy.

"You have to take risks in life!" says Sean mischievously.

"Don't you dare!" cries Mommy, reaching out to grab his sleeve.

Sean pushes her hand away, turns, and runs down the stairs.

"Daddy! Catch him!" Mommy yells as she struggles out of her seat.

Daddy jolts up. His cell phone is falling from his jacket pocket.

He scrambles to pick it up and dashes downstairs after Sean. He sees Sean stepping off the bus onto the sidewalk and manages to jump off after him at the last second. The bus doors close behind him.

Mommy doesn't make it outside. She stands on the exit landing, staring at them through the window.

"Please open the door, sir!" she calls to the bus driver anxiously.

The driver opens the door, and Mommy steps out and dashes furiously toward Sean.

Training Day Three

It's another beautiful summer day in London. The "Iniesta" team kids are on their lunch break. Sprawled on the grass, they cool off in a clearing beneath the shade of some oak trees. Sean sits some distance away from the group, not taking part in their happy chit-chat. He ties the laces of his worn-out cleats and turns to open the lunchbox Mommy packed for him.

Neil and Paul have just finished eating and are playing "water bottle flip."

"One, two, three, go!"

They throw their water bottles simultaneously. The bottles fly up, rotate in the air and land perfectly upright on their bottoms.

The kids shriek gleefully.

Nearby, Howard, one of the Taiwanese twins, turns to Shira and asks quietly, "Do you know when Diego is going to announce who's being picked for the La Masia Academy?"

Overhearing this, Paul, the English kid, bursts into laughter.

"It's not for the La Masia Academy. It's for the La Masia Tournament!" he yells.

Sean listens in attentively.

"What's the difference?" asks Howard.

"There's a tournament at La Masia with the best players from all the FC Barcelona soccer camps from all over the world. And Diego is going to pick me to join!" grins Paul cockily.

Neil turns to Howard. "Oh, Chi-chu!" he yells in a fake fearful voice, pointing at Howard's hair. "There's a spider on your head!"

Howard jerks, and his hands brush his hair in a panic. A roar of laughter spreads through the group of kids.

"Just ignore him," Sean says to Howard quietly.

At that moment, Benji, the coach, approaches.

"What's the joke, Team Iniesta? C'mon, your lunch break is over. Let's head back to the field. Give me a straight line, please."

The kids keep laughing.

"Chop, chop!" Benji calls. "Let's walk! Whoever is last is Ronaldo!"

Once again, a heated soccer game is on. Sean, Howard, Mathew, and Shira are on the White team, playing against the Yellow team, which includes Neil, Paul, Floris, and Oman.

The Yellows play mercilessly. Neil and Paul together on the same team are a big challenge. They don't give the Whites any opportunities. After ten minutes, the score is two to zero for the Yellows.

Frustrated, Sean dribbles toward the opposing goal. Neil is running his way, so he needs to make a quick decision. He searches for a free player. From the corner of his eye, he sees Diego, the Spanish coach, approaching their field.

"Control the ball! What's your next move, Sean?" yells Benji. "Formation, Whites! Where are my formations?"

The Whites move around, switching places on the field, but the Yellows' defense is too tight.

"No options?" calls Benji. "Pass to the goalie. He will know what to do."

As Neil charges at Sean, Sean manages to kick the ball back to Mathew, the goalie.

Then Neil crashes into Sean. His foot meets Sean's shin guard and knocks him off balance.

Sean falls, holding his aching shin, and tears well up in his eyes.

In the goal, Mathew is holding the ball above his head, searching for a free player. "Quickly, shape up, Whites!" yells Benji.

Sean shakes off the pain and scrambles to his feet.

Mathew throws the ball to Shira, who runs through the center of the field.

"Watch the middle, Yellows!" calls Benji.

From the sidelines, Diego is watching the action closely as well. Determined to impress, Sean, Howard, and Mathew run forward.

Shira passes to Sean. Sean receives and runs to the goal with all his might, Paul at his heels. He dribbles past Floris, toward the left, and achieves a clear line to the Yellows' goal. He knows he can score, but he sees Howard in a better position to the front right of the field. Howard raises his hand to signal that he is free. There's a split-second to decide. As Sean hesitates, Neil closes in on Howard.

At the last second, Sean kicks an exact pass to Howard, who, in turn, meets the ball in mid-air and shoots it just past Neil's head straight into the net.

"Goooooooooal!" shout the Whites. They jump ecstatically on Howard, hugging him and screaming in excitement. Howard is grinning, raising his two index fingers in the air in a Messi-style celebration.

"Good job!" Diego nods his head approvingly.

Howard makes eye contact with Sean and gives him a thumbs-up to show his gratitude.

"Beautiful goal!" yells Benji. "Bibs in piles! We're finished for today!"

Trouble On Oxford Street

Mommy looks out the balcony window of the apartment where they're staying. It's only late afternoon, but it's already grayish outside. The sky has turned gloomy and overcast. It seems like they are finally getting to experience typical London weather.

Daddy and Sean are taking turns in front of the full-length wall mirror. Sean is working on his dab goal celebration, and Daddy is trying on the clothes he's bought on Oxford Street. He inspects his reflection in the mirror.

"This shirt doesn't fit well. I need a smaller size. I want to go back and exchange it," he says.

"I'll come with you!" exclaims Sean enthusiastically.

"You can go, but no shopping for you. Your punishment for getting off the bus the other day still stands," Mommy reminds him.

"I know, I know," Sean agrees. "I will behave myself, I promise!"

"I hope you learned your lesson," says Daddy.

Mommy sighs. "I don't feel so well," she confesses. "I think I might be coming down with a little bit of a cold. Is it okay if I stay in the apartment and rest?"

Daddy looks at her worriedly. "Sure, get some rest. Tomorrow is an important day. You don't want to miss the camp closing ceremony. Would you like me to make you a cup of tea?"

"Yes, please," Mommy smiles. "But do you know how to get to Oxford Street without me?"

"Sure thing. Bus number fifty-five," Daddy replies confidently as he pours Mommy a cup of tea.

Mommy is still concerned. "If there's a problem, just give me a call," she says.

"I hope you feel better, Mommy!" Sean calls as they leave.

Sean and Daddy are in the clothing store changing room. Daddy has picked out a bunch of shirts and is trying one on.

"What do you think, Sean?" he asks as he glances in the mirror.

"It looks great on you, Daddy. Super cool."

Daddy is not convinced. He tries the next shirt in the pile.

"Daddy, do you think Diego will pick me for the world tournament?" asks Sean.

"I don't know, son."

A worried look appears on Sean's face. "Daddy, can I get the Messi haircut today?"

"Sean, Mommy said no."

"But, Daddy! You can't obey everything Mommy says."

Daddy huffs, annoyed. "I don't."

"It won't take long. We'll do it quickly." Sean won't give up.

"Sean! Your punishment isn't over until we leave London."

"But it's only about shopping. Haircuts don't count," Sean persists.

"Please stop nagging. I said no," concludes Daddy.

An hour later, Daddy and Sean step out of a hairdresser's, big smiles on their faces. Both have brand-new haircuts and platinum-bleached Mohawks. They inspect their surroundings.

"Which way, Daddy?" asks Sean, enjoying his new Messi look.

"Let's go back to Oxford Street and take bus fifty-five," Daddy says.

They walk in the direction they came, turning right at the corner. They stride down one busy street, then another. Everything looks the same. They can't find Oxford Street.

A light drizzle starts falling from the sky. Daddy contemplates which way to go.

"Call Mommy," advises Sean. "She will know what to do."

"No, we will manage," says Daddy decisively.

The light rain wets their hair and flattens their platinum Mohawks. Drops of rain dot their jacket shoulders.

Daddy stops under an awning. He hands Sean the shopping bags and searches his jacket pockets for his phone. No phone. He pats his pants pockets, too.

"I can't find my phone," he says finally.

"Oh, no!" cries Sean.

"It must have fallen from my pocket at some point," sighs Daddy.

"Should we go back and look for it?"

"I don't know. It was an old phone. And it's getting late."

"How are we going to get back, Daddy?" asks Sean, worried.

"Easy. We're staying in Islington, right? We can take any underground that goes south to King's Cross. I know the way from there."

"South? Are you sure?" presses Sean.

"You think it's north?" Daddy hesitates.

"Maybe not."

Daddy contemplates the matter for a second. Mommy's advice rings in his head. "Let's go north," he says finally.

Mommy puts down her book, takes the last sip from her fourth cup of tea, and wonders once more where Sean and Daddy are. It's been three hours since they left. They should have been back by now.

She picks up her phone and calls Daddy's number, but there's no answer.

Outside, it's getting dark and the drizzle has turned to light showers. Why aren't they back yet? Should she go look for them?

Mommy returns to her book, but she can't concentrate. After another half-hour, she tries to call Daddy again, but there's still no answer. "Why doesn't Daddy answer his phone?" she wonders.

Suddenly, her phone rings.

She jumps and grabs it. It's Daddy's number on the caller ID!

"Daddy!" she exclaims as she answers the call.

"Hello?" an uncertain young woman's voice replies.

"Yes?" Mommy says, confused, her heart fluttering in her chest.

"Hi...I found this phone. Does it belong to someone in your family?" asks the woman.

"Oh my god! It's my husband's phone. Where did you find it?" Mommy's voice falters.

"On bus fifty-five. About an hour ago. I'm sorry I didn't call before - I was in the middle of something."

"That's okay. You are an angel!"

"I called the last outgoing number," the woman explains. "I know how awful it is to lose a cell phone."

"Thank you so much for calling. My husband must have

accidentally dropped the phone."

The woman is very friendly and offers to meet Mommy the next evening to return the phone. She gives Mommy the directions.

Mommy hangs up the phone, and looks outside. The rain is now a chilly downpour. She opens the balcony door to look down at the street, but the rain splashes inside, so she closes it, shivering. Where are her boys?

Pacing back and forth in the apartment, Mommy ponders what should she do.

Suddenly, she hears commotion from behind the closed apartment door. She listens carefully. The noises come closer. She hears a key wiggle into the keyhole. She approaches and stares at the door. It opens slowly, and Sean's head, complete with wet platinum locks, pops into the room, a huge smile plastered across his face.

Mommy sighs in relief.

Daddy's drenched head appears next.

"What do you think of my hair, Mommy?" Daddy asks.

"You two went to get a haircut, after all!" Mommy laughs. "And you bleached it! Both of you!"

"Sean made me do it," Daddy says defensively.

"Sean made you?" Mommy is doubtful.

"Yes, and there's something else I need to tell you," Daddy adds hesitantly. "I lost my phone."

"There's something else I need to tell you, too," Mommy smiles. "I found your phone."

Closing Ceremony

The camp closing ceremony is set to take place at the Harrow indoor basketball arena, since rain continues falling on and off all the next day.

Arranged by their teams, excited kids in red uniforms stand at the far end of the hall. The coaches stand in a row in front of them. A delighted crowd of parents and family members awaits, as Coldplay's song "When I Ruled The World" plays loudly.

"FC Barcelona Camp" banners decorate the walls.

Mommy and Daddy are seated in the front row, Mommy's cell phone camera ready at hand to capture the moment.

The ceremony is about to begin.

The music is turned off and the camp manager comes out to the front and taps the mic to get everyone's attention.

"Welcome to London's FC Barcelona Camp closing ceremony," he says. "It's been a very productive week. Your kids have trained hard and learned many valuable lessons. I am very proud of all of them. Let's give them a hand." He claps his hands, and the audience joins him in a cheerful round of applause.

"First, we will hand out the certificates for completion of training," he continues, "and then Diego Alfaro, our guest coach from La Masia, Barcelona, will say a few final words."

The Barca anthem starts playing and everybody sings along.

Once it ends, the manager begins announcing each kid's name, starting with the youngest ones. One by one, each child approaches the row of coaches and shakes their hands. Last in the line of coaches, Diego gives each player a certificate. Then, each kid turns to the crowd and pauses for the cameras, proudly presenting the certificate with their name next to a photo of FC Barcelona's players.

Sean, Neil, Howard, Mathew, and the other "Iniesta" team members await their turn.

"Diego is going to pick me for the tournament, you'll see," whispers Neil to his teammates.

"Maybe…and maybe not," mumbles Howard.

"You keep quiet, Chi-Chu," Neil mocks.

"Neil Osborne!" they hear over the mic. Neil turns and rushes to the makeshift stage.

Sean's name is read next. He follows Neil to the stage and shakes the coaches' hands with a timid smile. When he approaches Benji, he overhears Diego say to Neil, "Good job!", as he gives him his certificate.

Sean's tummy ties itself in knots and tears well up in his eyes. Did Diego pick Neil for the tournament? It's not fair!

He tries to keep the smile on his face as he receives his

certificate from Diego.

"Sean!" He hears Mommy's voice calling.

He turns to look at his parents. Mommy is taking pictures with her phone, and Daddy is clapping his hands excitedly.

Sean steps back to where the rest of the "Iniesta" team stands.

"Did you hear what Diego just told me? I don't think your new Messi hairdo helped you," Neil says to him with a grin. "Now I'm sure Diego picked me for the tournament!"

Sean ignores him. He shrugs his shoulders and bites on his fingernails. Then he makes a decision.

Stepping away from the line, he approaches his gear bag, inserts the certificate, and pulls out his soccer ball. He holds it in front of him with both hands, assessing the distance to the basketball hoop on the wall, thirty feet away.

"One, two, three!" he calls loudly.

As he shouts, everyone looks his way, puzzled by this interruption. The camp manager stops reading names. Mommy and Daddy stare at Sean, baffled.

Sean kicks the ball toward the basketball hoop. The ball travels through the air and everyone follows it with their eyes. It hits the backboard, spins a few times on the hoop and falls through, landing on the floor with a thump.

A gasp of admiration sweeps through the crowd.

"Good job," mumbles Diego, nodding his head in appreciation.

Mommy's mouth hangs open in disbelief. Daddy holds his hands to his face.

In the silence that ensues, the camp manager mumbles confusedly into the mic. "Errrr...okay...."

Daddy recovers first. He claps his hands once, breaking the awkward silence. He claps again, and again, and again, and soon enough, a round of enthusiastic applause fills the room.

"Um......okay...that was....interesting," the camp manger says into the mic. "Now, let us carry on with the ceremony."

"Shira Silva," he reads the next name. Shira steps forward and the ceremony continues.

"If this was a basketball game, that would have been three points!" Howard whispers to Sean, giggling.

Neil looks at them indignantly.

Once all the certificates have been handed out, Diego steps up to the mic to give his speech. The kids hold their breath. Sean chews his fingernails nervously. Neil clenches his fists. Howard closes his eyes and breathes deeply.

"Hello, everyone!" begins Diego. "I hope you enjoyed our London summer camp. It was a wonderful experience for me. I saw a lot of talent and hard work here, in the true Barca spirit. Together, we worked on many aspects of the game: technical precision, game intelligence, and of course, teamwork. As you may know, The La Masia Soccer Academy is the heart of FC Barcelona. There are not many clubs in the world with so much home-grown talent. Messi, Xavi, Iniesta, Pique, and other famous Barcelona first team players spent many years as students at La Masia. This is our pride. This is our philosophy."

A round of applause fills the room. Sean claps his hands feebly and glances nervously at his parents.

"It takes years to become a skillful soccer player," continues Diego. "But you kids are well on your way. You are on the right path. Just continue training hard, and keep practicing the Barca way!"

Diego waits until another round of applause subsides.

"Now, I've heard that some of you have it in your heads that we will pick players from this camp for the La Masia World Tournament, but I am sorry to say that is not the case. The spots for this year are already filled. Sorry to disappoint you." He sighs. "However, I saw a lot of amazing talent here, and there's always next year. Keep growing and learning, and I hope to see you again at our camps, here in London, or in Barcelona. Thank you and goodbye!"

The music is turned back on, and Coldplay's song "When I Ruled The World" overtakes the noise of the crowd's clapping.

Neil is devastated.

Sean looks at Howard disappointedly and says, "Next year?"

"Next year," agrees Howard.

Who's The Captain?

Sean and Mommy are seated in adjacent seats on the underground. The train rattles as it hurries through tunnels to the next station. They are exhausted after all of the week's excitement. Daddy stands near them, holding Sean's backpack. Sean looks at the people around him. Some stare blankly, some play with their phones, some listen to music. He tries to guess who they are and where they're going.

"So, what did you think about the camp, Sean?" Mommy asks.

"It was awesome," he replies.

"That stunt you pulled at the ceremony? It was definitely something," she tells her son.

"Neil didn't deserve to get picked by Diego," Sean says. "Was it very bad what I did?"

"Not bad, no...Creative, I would say." Mommy chooses her words carefully.

"Can we go again next year?" asks Sean.

"Where are we going now?" Daddy interrupts the conversation.

"We take the blue line and then we switch to the red line," Mommy explains.

"But where to?" asks Daddy.

"I'm not sure exactly...The woman who found your phone gave me directions. We are meeting her at her bookstore."

Daddy smiles at her. "Okay. I trust you, Mommy. You know your way around."

Sean runs up the underground stairs to the street. Mommy and Daddy clamber behind him, squinting their eyes against the bright sun. The weather has changed and it's a beautiful day once again. The air is fresh, and the leaves on the trees sparkle in the sun.

They look around them.

"We're in Notting Hill!" cries Daddy happily. "How cool is that!"

From somewhere nearby, they hear bass beats. They walk down the street, past trendy coffee shops, quirky secondhand stores, Moroccan tea houses, and fast-food places.

As they proceed, the music gets louder and the crowd around them gets denser. They reach a pedestrian street with a flea market. Street vendors are selling all kinds of tasty snacks.

They find the woman's bookstore next to where a DJ is set up. People are dancing around an improvised stage. Inside the bookstore, they meet the store owner - the woman who found Daddy's phone. She wears a colorful dress and shakes her body to the beat of the music as she calls over to them, "This is your lucky day! We're having a street party! You have to join us!"

The woman hands Daddy his phone. He thanks her and they follow her outside to join the party.

Daddy begins to move to the beat of the music as works his way between the dancing bodies, a big smile on his face. Sean grabs Daddy's hand and begins dancing, too.

Mommy looks at them and laughs in delight.

"Come on, Mommy! Come dance with us! Don't be shy!" calls Daddy.

Mommy smiles and walks toward them hesitantly. She begins to dance timidly, but, soon enough, she too is carried away by the music.

They dance together in the crowd of young and old smiling faces of all colors, happy people enjoying life and sunshine and the brilliant London summer.

"Look at us! We're dancing together! We are a team!" shouts Daddy.

"Yes," Sean calls, "and I am the captain!"

END OF BOOK 3

To be continued...

To check out the other books
in the series and get notified when
the next book is coming visit:
sean-wants-to-be-messi.com

Made in the USA
Middletown, DE
22 November 2020

24820738R00035